Published by Sweet Cherry Publishing Limited
Unit 36, Vulcan House,
Vulcan Road,
Leicester, LE5 3EF
United Kingdom

First published in the US in 2019
2019 edition

2 4 6 8 10 9 7 5 3 1

ISBN: 978-1-78226-554-2

© Stella Tarakson

Hopeless Heroes: Apollo's Mystic Message!

Cover design by Nick Roberts and Rhiannon Izard
Illustrations by Nick Roberts

www.sweetcherrypublishing.com

Printed and bound in India
I.TP002

For my son, James,

for being full of ideas

"Dessert's ready!" Tim Baker's mother called from the kitchen. The smell of freshly baked apple pie drifted up the stairs, through Tim's open door, and into his room. Mom's too-cheery voice sounded strained and forced. Tim thought he knew why.

As far as Mom knew, he and her boyfriend Larry – an Australian who was a teacher at Tim's school – were having a man-to-man talk about how they would get along together. Mom wanted so much for Tim and the teacher to like each other. This was the first time that she'd had a boyfriend since Tim's father died. He could tell she was nervous about it. So was he.

In a way, it was true: Tim and Larry *were* working out how they would get along. What Mom didn't know, however, was how they were doing it. She didn't know that Tim had told Larry his biggest secret. She didn't know what that secret was – or even that he had one.

Tim had told Larry that he could time travel to and from Ancient Greece. He hadn't been boasting or trying to impress the teacher. Far from it: Tim had no choice. It was either trust Larry and ask for help, or let down his friend Zoe when she needed him the most.

Zoe was the daughter of the Greek hero who'd been trapped in Mom's vase. Hercules had been imprisoned by Hera, the spiteful queen goddess of Olympus, for thousands of years until Tim accidentally broke the vase and freed him. That same vase now allowed Tim to travel through time and have adventures. But freeing the hero had angered Hera. She was determined to recapture Hercules, and didn't much like Tim and Zoe getting in the way. Her

latest punishment had been to trap Zoe in a giant puzzle prison.

Larry was the only person who could solve the puzzle and let Zoe out – so Tim had asked for his help. Luckily, the teacher turned out to be unflappable and kind of cool. Everything had been fine and they'd returned home safe

and sound, where Larry had turned so pale that Tim wondered if he'd suddenly become ill or seen a ghost. It wasn't either of those things. The teacher had recalled something he'd seen at the

British Museum. Something that had the experts puzzled …

It was a recently discovered Ancient Greek oil flask. Strangely, it seemed to have a drawing of a boy wearing a modern school uniform. Knowing what he now did about Tim's adventures, Larry thought it might be a picture of Tim.

"I'm sorry, mate, but I don't think you should time travel anymore," Larry said, his green eyes glittering. "You might be changing history – you *are* changing history. After all, if you hadn't visited the past, that flask wouldn't exist."

Tim shrugged. "It's only a picture on a pot. How does that change anything?"

"The thing is, we just don't know." Larry perched on the edge of Tim's bed and stretched out his long legs. "Think of it like this: you throw a pebble in a pond and it makes a small splash. But it doesn't end there. It creates ripples, and they spread. Have you ever heard of the butterfly effect?"

Tim looked back blankly. What did butterflies have to do with pebbles? Or ponds, for that matter.

"A butterfly flaps its wings in China," Larry

said, flapping his fingers. "A week later, a tornado hits America. Did the butterfly's wings cause the tornado?"

Tim gaped. Was the man crazy? Maybe the adventure had been too much for him!

Larry, guessing what Tim was thinking, smiled weakly. "It's a math idea called chaos theory. Small things can lead to big changes, in ways that are hard to predict."

"It's only a picture—"

"A picture that shouldn't exist," Larry cut in firmly. "How many times have you visited the past?"

Tim tried to do a quick calculation in his head but failed. "Um, not many …" He scrunched his face in thought. "I didn't see any butterflies, though," he added helpfully.

Larry blinked. "OK … But already things have changed. And what about me? Flashing my mobile phone around like that! I shouldn't have flaunted it in the ancient world."

"You had to," Tim said, remembering

 how frightened Hera had been of the modern technology. With it, Larry had convinced the goddess that he had magical powers she couldn't hope to

understand. It was only her confusion that had allowed them to escape.

"Ripples in time," Larry said darkly. "Tiny changes that spread and grow, over thousands of years. If you keep going back, the effect could get bigger and bigger. It could change the present in ways we'd never expect."

"But if I'm extra careful …"

"NO, TIM."

Larry pressed his lips together. "It's started already."

"It might not be me on the flask!" Tim protested. "Maybe you've got it wrong! You'd be spoiling everything for nothing."

"Coffee's going cold!" Mom's voice floated up the stairs.

"Tell you what," Larry said, standing up and walking to the door. "You've got a trip to the British Museum next week, right? I've been assigned to help. We'll look at the flask together. If it isn't a picture of you, well, then it might be okay."

A week was an awfully long time to wait.

"You couldn't take me before then, could you?" Tim asked as they went down the stairs. "Maybe this weekend?"

"Not a good idea, mate. Your mom and I aren't ready to go public yet."

"What isn't a good idea?" Mom met them in the hallway and ushered them into the kitchen. Her brow furrowed as she spoke.

"All's good, Penny, don't worry,"
Larry reassured her. "We've reached an
understanding."

"Can you take me to the British
Museum this weekend, Mom?"

She shook her head as she slid a piece
of apple pie and a glass of milk before
Tim. "I've got too much work. My
deadline's approaching. Anyway, aren't
you going with school?
Why go twice?"

She looked from Tim to Larry and back again.

Tim knew not to push it. Mom would ask too many awkward questions.

"Oh, yeah. I forgot."

"There we are then. You can wait." Mom nodded, satisfied. "How much ice cream do you want with your pie?"

"How much have you got?" Larry said, and grinned.

Tim knew the teacher was trying to make him feel better. But not even ice cream could calm the butterflies in his stomach.

The week passed slowly, but finally
the day of the trip arrived. Tim had to
remember to call Larry "Mr. Green" in
front of the other kids – especially if
Leo the bully was around. The last thing
Tim needed was for Leo to figure out
that the teacher was seeing Tim's mother.
Tim knew from hard experience that if
Leo smelled a mystery, he wouldn't stop
prying.

Leo enjoyed upsetting Tim. He was
the one who'd come up with the annoying
nickname "Cinderella." All because Tim
had to do the housework! It wasn't his
fault Mom had to work two jobs, leaving
him to do the chores.

"Hey everyone, watch. What's this?"
Leo pulled a tissue out of his pocket and
pretended to dust a sarcophagus in the

Egypt room. Heads swiveled, but Tim gritted his teeth and stared straight ahead. He could guess what was coming.

"Cinderella at home with his mummy!" Leo brayed, wobbling with mirth.

All of the kids laughed except for Tim and his best friend Ajay. "Ignore him," Ajay said, dark eyes flashing. "Act like you didn't notice."

"What's the matter?" Leo sidled up to them. "That comment was pharaoh-nuff! *Pharaoh*-nuff! Get it? Like *fair enough*?

HAH!"

Ajay fixed Leo with a hard stare. "I wouldn't get too close to that mummy if I were you," he said, his voice deadpan. "There's a curse on it. Last time someone touched it, their freckles fell off."

Leo's hand automatically strayed to his cheek, but then he scowled. "Yeah, very funny. You need to watch it before someone messes you up."

"Come on, boys, keep moving." Their class teacher Miss Omiros shooed them along as Larry strode ahead. "There's a lot to get through."

Normally Tim would be interested in everything, but today he only had eyes for Greek pottery. He passed the Egyptian and Assyrian exhibits with barely a glance. Finally, they reached the room with the Greek vases. Tim snapped his head around, trying to take it all in at once. He only succeeded in making himself dizzy.

Larry coughed and caught his eye. The teacher nodded toward a glass cabinet in the center of the room. Folding his arms casually, Larry moved behind Tim as he crossed to

the display. There, on a high shelf, was a slender flask. Tim had to stand on his toes to get a better look.

Only about a foot tall, it was much smaller than his magic vase. The flask had a single loop-shaped handle and a narrow neck. A band of intricate decorations circled the flask, but Tim's gaze shot straight to the figure etched on the white background. His eyes bulged.

The boy was dressed exactly like him.

Tim glanced down at his school uniform: pants, shirt, blazer, tie. Nobody in Ancient Greece dressed like that. They believed only barbarians wore pants. And ties – surely they hadn't even been invented yet.

Most worrying was the fact that the boy was holding a vase. It was identical to Tim's, right down to the picture of Hercules wrestling a bull on the front.

Larry pointed at a printed sheet of paper next to the flask. Tim craned his neck for a closer look.

UNSOLVED MYSTERY

This new find has stirred a great deal of interest among archaeologists. The white-ground lekythos — or oil flask — is typical of the type used as grave gifts in Attica. Dated circa 540-480 BC, this flask is unusual in its decoration. Most depict burial rites and the journey to the afterlife of the deceased. This figure, however, seems to be wearing modern dress. Tagged the Time Traveler's Flask, the find has sparked debate. Accusations of hoaxes have been made, yet all analyses so far indicate that this is a genuine article.

Gulping, Tim turned away. The words "grave gifts" and "burial rites" echoed through his skull like a tolling bell.

"Whaddya looking at, Cinderella?" Leo asked, pushing in front of Tim to see what had caught his interest.

"I'd get rid of those jelly beans if I were you, Leo," Larry said, without even glancing at the boy. "If I see you sneak one out of your pocket again, I'll confiscate the whole bag."

Leo scuttled away, but Tim felt no sense of triumph. He looked at the teacher, who frowned and shook his head.

"See what I mean? It's you." Larry spoke under his breath, so that nobody else could hear.

"I've changed the past," Tim whispered. Images of butterflies and tornadoes spun through his head.

"I'm afraid so," Larry said, frowning.

Suddenly a thought occurred to Tim and he gasped. Larry looked at him questioningly.

"The vase that Hera trapped Hercules in had his picture on it. This has my picture on it …" Tim swallowed as he put two and two together. "Does that mean … Is Hera after *me* now?"

Larry looked down at Tim in surprise. "Of course Hera's after you. Hasn't she always been?"

"Yes, but this time it feels different," Tim insisted.

"In what way?"

How could Tim explain? Previously, Hera had tried to stop Tim and Zoe from protecting Hercules so that she could capture him again. She'd never gone directly for Tim before.

"The other times, it was to stop us from interfering with her plans," he said. "But now – well, I'm not doing anything! I'm not even there, and Hera's coming after me anyway. I just don't know why."

Sighing, Larry scratched the stubble on his chin. "That settles it. You can't go back to Ancient Greece."

"But I have to!" Tim squeaked.

"Why?" Larry moved aside to allow a family to squeeze past him.

"Why?" Tim echoed, rooted to the spot. "B-because I have to! Zoe and Hercules will wonder why I haven't gone back! They'll worry about me."

"Sssh. Don't attract attention." Larry steered Tim around to the other side of the display case, where there were fewer people.

A thought occurred to Tim and he peered at the back of the flask. The writing on Hercules' vase had been put there by his father Zeus to give the demigod a way to escape. Unlike Hercules' vase, the back of this flask was worryingly blank. By the look of it, nobody had tried to help Tim escape.

Tim continued to stare at the flask. Although old and chipped, it was intact – not broken and glued back together. His thoughts trailed down an unsettling path. That must mean that if he *had* become trapped ... the vase was never broken ...

and he had never escaped! He gulped. "Do you think– Is it possible that …"

"What?" Larry asked.

Tim lowered his voice to a whisper. "Do you suppose I'm actually *inside* it? Like, right now?"

"WHAT?"

Larry's eyebrows shot to the top of his head. "You can't be, mate. You're standing here."

But Tim, who was more used to the trickiness of time travel, wasn't so sure. What if something was going to happen in his personal future? Hera might trap a *future* Tim in the flask, and his present self would have no idea! Hadn't something like that happened on *Doctor Who*? If he could look inside the flask, he might see a tiny Tim peering out!

"Do you think they'd open the case and let us look inside?" Tim asked.

"No." Larry was emphatic. "Look, I can't pretend to understand the paradoxes of time travel any more than you do. All I know is that it's safer to stay put. It feels like a warning. Hera's angry, but if you don't go back, you won't provoke her. Then all the flask is good for is confusing archaeologists. Right?"

Tim couldn't disagree with the logic. "Right."

"So don't go back and you'll be safe. Right?"

Unfortunately, Tim couldn't come up with an argument against that.

Tim was subdued for the rest of the trip. He barely even reacted when Leo picked up a fridge-magnet owl in the museum's gift shop and swooped it in Tim's direction. "Make sure you're

£1.50   75p

home by midnight, Cinderella, or your carriage will turn back into an owl!"

"Pumpkin," Tim corrected him mildly.

"Is it?" Leo paused mid-swoop, then snickered, "I don't give a hoot! Get it?

HOOT!"

The class giggled obediently, but Tim didn't care. He had bigger problems. Problems that nagged him right through the day and into the afternoon, when he was back at home looking for the dustcloth. Tim had let the housework slide lately. Too many distractions. All that traveling to Greece and meeting heroes. All of those adventures …

They were all over now, though. He
might as well accept it.

"Have you seen the dustcloth?" Tim
asked the tiger-skin rug half-heartedly. The
rug hadn't been the same since Hercules
had tried to wrestle it. Untidy stitch marks
ran down the length of the tiger skin's
body where Tim had sewn it back together.
It gazed back through glazed eyes.

"I don't blame you if you don't feel like
talking," Tim said. "I'd be upset, too, if I
were covered in stitches." He sighed. "But
nothing else will happen now. Life's going

back to normal. I suppose that's for the best." Another giant sigh racked his body.

Tim got on his hands and knees and peered under the sofa. Maybe the dustcloth was under there. He couldn't see it, but he did see something else. It was shiny and sort of tube-shaped. Something must have fallen and got wedged under there. Tim slid his hand in the gap but couldn't quite reach it.

"Can you see what it is?" he asked the tiger-skin rug, who had a better vantage point. "No?" Tim clambered back up, brushing off the dust. "I know. I'll get a stick or something." He ran into the kitchen and came back with a wooden spoon. "This'll do."

Tim knelt down and slid the spoon under the sofa. He jiggled it until it hit the object with a low chiming sound. Tim deftly fished it out. It looked like a slender ceramic bottle with a handle. Not daring to breathe, Tim used the spoon to gently turn it over.

"*AARGH!*"

Tim sprang back in alarm. It was a Greek oil flask – just like the one in the museum!

It even had the same picture of Tim in his school uniform. How did the flask get here? Had it followed him?

No. Don't be silly. Tim tried to settle his beating heart. This flask couldn't be the British Museum's flask. That one was chipped and worn and thousands of years old. This one looked brand new – as if it had traveled through time … straight from Ancient Greece.

Tim eyed the flask like he would a deadly snake. "What does it mean?" he asked the tiger-skin rug in a whisper. It didn't reply.

Late that night, Tim awoke with a jerk. He tried to figure out what had disturbed him. It wasn't the morning sun. It wasn't his alarm. He peered at the digital display. 2 a.m. He'd never been up so early before. Another five hours until his alarm was due to go off, yet he felt totally awake. Groaning, he rolled over and tried to go back to sleep.

His brain wouldn't let him.

It kept thinking about the oil flask he'd found in the living room the day before. Tim had been about to pick up the little flask and throw it away when a strong feeling told him not to. Touching it with his bare hands seemed like a bad idea somehow. He'd wrapped it in an old brown towel and thrown the entire bundle into the trash. Hopefully Mom wouldn't notice the towel was missing.

But Mom getting angry over a threadbare towel was the least of his worries. The flask was just like the one in the museum, except it looked brand new. Hera was reaching out to capture him whether he was around to "provoke" her or not. Staying put in the modern world

didn't seem so safe anymore. Was he
better off avoiding Ancient Greece, or was
visiting it the only way he could find help?
Even after an entire evening of thinking,
Tim was no nearer to an answer.

An owl hooted outside Tim's window.
Maybe that's what woke him. Tim heard
a rustle of wings, and he glanced at the
window, hoping to catch a glimpse of the
bird. That was when he saw the reflection
in the glass: a shimmer of golden sparkles,
illuminating a floating figure. Snapping
his head around, Tim saw a young man
dressed in a white chiton, with wings
on his cap and sandals, appearing in the
middle of his room.

Hermes.

"Hey!" Tim yelped.

Hermes looked down at him. A grin lit the messenger god's face. "Shh. You'll wake your mom."

"What's happening?" Tim asked, gripping his blanket. "Do you know about the flask? Yesterday I saw—"

"You saw nothing," the god said soothingly. "You're dreaming."

"But—"

Quicker than a heartbeat, Hermes vanished. Tim sat up in bed, shaking. Had he imagined the whole thing? Maybe his befuddled brain had confused the sound of the owl's flight with Hermes' wings. Maybe.

But Tim didn't think so.

Being the messenger god, Hermes was the only Greek god who could travel freely outside of Ancient Greece. He'd helped Tim once or twice, but Tim still didn't know if he could trust him. Hermes served Hera. Once, he'd even brought the goddess to Tim's house so that she could steal the magic vase from under Tim's nose.

Heart pounding, Tim switched on his bedside lamp. Squinting, he peered around his room: at his chair, his desk, his cricket bat leaning against the wall; at the sheet-draped vase that peeped out of his open wardrobe. It was still there – thankfully – and everything looked normal. Nothing was missing, as far as he could tell. So what had Hermes been up to?

That did it. There was no way Tim would get back to sleep now. He was too wound up. Perhaps a glass of milk would help.

Tim swung his feet to the floor, kicking a slipper as he did so. A clinking noise startled him. The slipper had bumped against something under his bed. Watching his step, Tim climbed out of bed and squatted down. There was definitely something there, near

the edge. Something shiny and sort of tube-shaped …

"The flask again!" Tim squeaked.

How was that possible? He'd put it in the trash – he remembered it distinctly. Had it been moved? There was only one way to find out. Tim pulled on his slippers. He padded softly down the stairs, taking care not to wake Mom. Quietly he crept to the wastebasket and opened it. The old brown towel was there, all right. But it was lying loose and limp. It wasn't wrapped around anything. The flask had been taken – and placed under Tim's bed, where he could easily have stepped on it.

Tim dashed back up to his bedroom. Grabbing his cricket bat, he carefully

nudged the flask out from under his bed
and wrapped it in one of his t-shirts
to muffle the sound of what he was
about to do. Using all his strength, he
swung the bat down hard.

WHAM!

The force traveled
back up Tim's arm,
making his whole
body vibrate. The
flask was undamaged.
It was stronger than it
looked.

Suddenly, Tim *knew*.
Staying in the present
wouldn't protect him

from Hera's wrath. She was clearly already doing all she could to capture Tim.

He had to do something. There was no point in talking to Larry about it – he would insist that Tim stay put. Tim realized there was no choice: he had to go back to Ancient Greece. His friends understood Hera and her tricks better than anyone. They might know how to get rid of the flask.

Tim hauled the vase out of the wardrobe. He was about to grab its handles when a thought hit him. He didn't want Mom to touch the flask either. She might get trapped instead of him! Using the cricket bat, Tim pushed the flask as far under the bed as it would go, right up against the wall. The only way Mom would touch it was if she moved his bed – and why would she? Satisfied, Tim put the bat away.

"Oh vase," he intoned, gripping its handles. "Take me to Zoe's house."

Tim was starting to enjoy the rushing, whooshing sensation of traveling through time. It gave him a dizzy kind of thrill, and he thought he was well and truly used to it. But now, as the vase deposited him on Zoe's doorstep, he was jolted by a surprise.

It was the middle of the night. The usually bustling town was silent and still. There was no reason for Tim to be surprised that he'd arrived at nighttime. Obviously they had night in Ancient Greece, too. It was just that every time he'd visited so far, he'd arrived in broad daylight. Tim was amazed by how dark it was. There was no constant glow of electric streetlights. And the sky! He gazed up at the incredible array of stars, stretching out across the sky like a spreading puddle of milk.

Tim hesitated at Zoe's front door. He felt bad about waking his friends, but on the other hand, he didn't want to hang around for hours waiting for sunrise. He knocked softly.

"Psst!" he hissed. "Zoe. It's me. Let me in."

A flickering light flared through the cracks around the door. Tim heard the approach of heavy footsteps. Not Zoe, he guessed. The door was flung open and a massive figure glowered down at him. It was Hercules – but not as Tim had ever seen him before.

Hercules was wearing a loose ankle-length gown, a bit like an old-fashioned nightshirt. His curly hair was in disarray, and his bristly beard jutted out in all directions. In one hand he clutched a flaming torch, which he lowered so that he could peer into Tim's face. In the other he was holding a … could it be a giant teddy bear? It was some sort of stuffed toy the size of a Labrador.

"TIM BAKER!"

Hercules said through a jaw-cracking yawn. "What brings you here during the night? Are you in danger?" The hero poked his head out and looked around, alarmed.

"Sorry, I didn't realize–"

"Everyone is asleep. Keep your voice down!" Hercules boomed. "You'd better come inside."

The hero led Tim across the internal courtyard and into the house. He hooked the torch onto a bracket in the wall, flooding the room with rosy light.

"Is that a teddy bear?" Tim asked, unable to tear his eyes away from the toy.

"A what? Your words make no sense to me." Hercules followed Tim's gaze. "Oh, this? This is a votive owl. The goddess Athena gave it to me. She said it was very important. Something about it being sacred … I cannot remember exactly … but I have discovered an excellent use for it! It is most comforting during the night." He squeezed the giant owl affectionately, then held it out to Tim. "Would you like to cuddle it?"

"Err, no thanks." The owl was almost as big as Tim and looked unnervingly realistic. That was the third owl he'd come across in recent days, he realized. The fridge magnet in the British Museum, the owl at his window, and now this. Odd.

A scurrying of light footsteps told him that Zoe was awake.

"Tim!" she said joyfully as she burst into the room. Like her father, she was dressed in a loose ankle-length gown. Zoe looked at Tim and burst out laughing. "My gods, what are you wearing?"

Tim looked down at his pajamas. They were bright blue and covered with pictures of fluffy white bunnies. Tim blushed. He'd had them since he was little. The arms and legs were much too short, but they still fitted around the middle, so Mom had seen no need to replace them.

"Pyjamas," he said in a dignified manner. "For sleeping in."

"What are those strange drawings?" Zoe was peering at the cartoonish figures with a look of utter incomprehension.

"Never mind what they are," Agatha said, entering the room. Her long, fair hair was flowing loose down her back and she was suppressing a smile. "In the morning I'll find something else for you to wear. But for now, we'll make up a bed for you. You should get some sleep."

"OH, MA!"

Zoe complained. "He just got here! I haven't seen him in ages. We have a lot to catch up on." Tim could tell that his friend was burning with curiosity over his nighttime visit.

"There'll be plenty of time for that in the morning," Agatha said firmly.

Surrendering to a giant yawn, Tim couldn't help but agree.

. . .

"BREAKFAST!"

Agatha's musical voice stirred Tim from his sleep. Feeling rested, he jumped off the couch that had been his bed for the night. Tim couldn't wait to try an Ancient Greek breakfast. He didn't know what they ate, but it had to be more interesting than cornflakes.

Zoe, Hercules and Agatha were sitting at a wooden table. An array of food was spread out and Tim looked at it with interest. He sat next to Zoe and picked up a piece of bread. It was solid, and heavier than he expected. He nibbled the edge experimentally.

"Ouch!" The bread was rock hard.

"Tim," Zoe reprimanded him,

laughing. "Don't forget to dunk the barley-bread first. In the kylix." She demonstrated by dipping her bread in a wide-bowled ceramic cup. A ruby liquid stained the bread and the odor of alcohol drifted out.

"Wine?" Tim said, startled. "Kids drink wine here? Um, can I have water instead?"

Zoe looked surprised, but Agatha handed Tim a drinking vessel filled only with water.

"The food of Tim Baker's time is different," Hercules said knowledgeably. "They have an amazing variety, and all in little packages, too! I particularly miss potato chips. Do you think you could bring me a few packets next time?"

"Err …" Tim remembered what Larry had told him. Could potato chips really change history? If butterflies could cause tornadoes, anything was possible!

"Have some figs and nuts," Agatha invited, seeing him hesitate. "Or try the cheese and honey."

The cheese looked like ricotta, and was creamy and delicious. Tim ate his fill and drank the water, which tasted clean and fresh. As they ate, Tim told them about finding the oil flask with his picture on it.

"I don't know why she's suddenly targeting me like this," he said, licking honey off his lips.

Hercules cleared his throat. "I don't mean to offend you, Tim Baker, but I think it is *me* she is really after." He jabbed a sticky thumb at his chest. "*I'm* the important one here."

"You think this is just another attempt to capture you, Dad?" Zoe looked worried.

"It doesn't sound like it," Agatha said. She stood up and started to clear away the food. "I think Tim is right to be worried."

"And if I *did* get trapped, how would any of you even know?" Tim added. "I mean, you'd just think I hadn't had a chance to visit."

Zoe frowned. "Oh. Good point."

"So what can I do to stop her?" Tim asked, looking from face to face across the table.

"LET'S ASK APOLLO!"

Zoe said, her eyes glowing. "I've been meaning to get his autograph for ages. His band is the best!"

"Band?" Tim asked, puzzled. Was she referring to the god Apollo, or someone else?

"Apollo and the Muses. They're so cool! I just love their song *Losing My Marbles Over You*." She hummed a few bars of a jaunty, if somewhat aggressive, tune.

"Apollo's the god of music," Agatha told Tim. "He's also the god of prophecy, so maybe he *is* the right one to ask. Even though … What do you think, darling? Would Apollo's advice help keep Tim safe?" She turned to Hercules, who was busy finishing off a fistful of figs.

"Mmpf," he said, which sounded a bit like yes.

"Before you go …" Agatha said. She handed Tim a small bundle of cream-colored fabric. Tim unfolded it, his eyes glowing. His very own chiton! Now he'd look like a real Ancient Greek! He held the short tunic up against his chest and grinned.

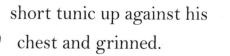

"Better than *that*," Zoe said, eyeing Tim's gaudy pajamas and collapsing in a fit of giggles.

Tim was relieved to be out of his
bunny pajamas. He was less likely
to be changing the past if he looked
like a real Ancient Greek. Even so, he
didn't feel much better in his chiton. It
felt alarmingly like he was wearing a
minidress. Agatha had given him a pair
of sandals, too, to replace his slippers. It
had taken Tim a while to figure out how
to put everything on.

Amazingly, Zoe hadn't laughed at his appearance. She stared at his pale, skinny legs, but said nothing. Tim suspected that Agatha had told her not to make any personal remarks. He also thought she might be the reason Hercules had agreed to let Tim and Zoe leave the house alone.

Apollo's temple was only a short walk away, but Tim wondered how they'd recognize it. He soon found out. Most temples in Ancient Greece were white and decorated with vivid red and blue panels and carvings. The temple ahead of them, however, was black — just black.

Tim came to a halt and stared at it, open-mouthed. He would have expected a black temple to be grim. Instead it sparkled and shone, as if it were built of polished gemstones.

"Is that it?" he gaped, pointing at the temple.

"Yeah, isn't it cool? Apollo is so awesome. I can't wait to meet him." Zoe led the way up the black marble steps.

"Hey, what's this say?" Tim pointed to a large clay tablet that was leaning against one of the columns. It was covered with jagged writing. Tim remembered that Zoe, unlike many girls of her time, could read.

"Oh, wow," she breathed, her eyes glued to the sign.

"What?" Tim prompted.

Zoe's voice shook as she read the words out.

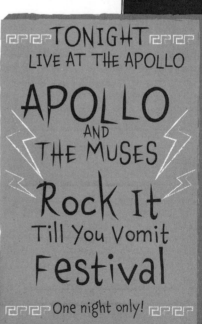

୮ଥ୮ଥ୮ଥ **TONIGHT** ୮ଥ୮ଥ୮ଥ
LIVE AT THE APOLLO

APOLLO
AND
THE MUSES

Rock It
Till You Vomit
Festival

୮ଥ୮ଥ୮ଥ One night only! ୮ଥ୮ଥ୮ଥ

"Maybe he'll give us free tickets!" Running ahead of Tim, Zoe darted through the temple's columns.

"Hey! Move it!" someone growled at her.

"Sorry, I–"

"Yeah, get out of the way, girlie!" said another voice.

Tim chased after Zoe to see what was wrong. He nearly bumped into two burly men carrying a large musical instrument between them. It looked like a cross between a harp and a guitar. The men's chitons were ripped and dirty, their faces hostile.

"Jeez, not another one!" the first man said when Tim entered. "This place is teeming with brats. Get outta here!"

"We've come to see Apollo," Zoe said.

"You'll be lucky," the man said, sneering. "He's busy. Didn't ya see the sign? Put it down here," he added to the second man as they grappled the instrument to the floor.

"I have to see Apollo," Zoe said primly. "My father sent me. He'll be furious if you refuse."

"Daddy wants an autograph, does he? Well, tough." The first man spat on the floor, then turned his back on them. "Where's he want those panpipes?" he asked his friend.

"I am the daughter of Hercules!" Zoe quivered indignantly. "And who are you?"

"We're Apollo's roadies, darlin', and you're in our way. Move it!"

"I must insist." Zoe folded her arms across her chest and stood her ground.

"Oh, listen to her! La di da! Get outta here, kid."

Tim couldn't help but admire his determined friend, but he gripped her arm and tugged. "Let's go. We'll think of something else."

"WHAT THE HADES IS GOING ON?"

A thundering voice flooded the temple and echoed through its chambers. "I'm trying to relax before my gagging gig!" An angry figure stalked toward them, a scowl on his flushed face.

The painfully
thin young man
was wearing silver-
studded sandals and a
ragged black chiton. His
bleached-white hair was
swept up in a massive
mohawk that looked sharp
enough to slice cheese.

"Sorry, Apollo," said
one of the roadies,
jerking his thumb at Zoe.
"We told this brat to beat
it, but she won't go."

"If you've woken me
up for an autograph
you're in for a world

of plague," Apollo sneered down his nose at the children. "I'm anti-autographs. They make me wanna puke my guts out!"

This was a god? Tim knew he shouldn't be surprised by anything anymore, but he'd never expected to come across an ancient punk.

"That's okay Mr. … um … Mr. Apollo, sir," he said. "We're not autograph hunters. We were after some advice. A prophecy, really. You see, I'm in danger, and I need to know how to protect myself–"

"I don't do no prophecies no more! I'm sick to the Styx of people pestering me, whinging and whining for advice. Get that through your *bile-brained* heads."

Apollo was so angry, wisps of thick black smoke curled out of his ears and drifted up to the ceiling.

"Coooool!" Zoe breathed.

"But – aren't you the god of prophecy?" Tim was bold enough to ask.

"So what?" Apollo's mohawk sliced through the air as he jerked his head. "I'm anti any of you wretches telling me what to do.

I'M A GOD! YEAH!"

He pumped his fist in the air, first and last fingers raised to make the shape of horns.

"Yeah!" Cheering, the roadies copied Apollo.

"You're my favorite rock star, Apollo, and it's such a thrill to meet you," Zoe simpered. "I love your new song *Puking on the Parthenon*. It's as good as your chart buster *Punk Odyssey*."

Tim looked at her in wonder. Did nothing put her off?

"Yeah. Well." Apollo wiped his nose on his forearm. "Reckon you got good taste an' all. But that don't change a vommy thing. Go away. I'm trying to relax."

Tim thought Apollo would find life far more relaxing if he stopped shouting, but he wisely decided to remain silent.

Zoe's flattery must have worked, though, because the angry god seemed to relent somewhat.

"Look – go see my oracle, she can spew the prophecy. That's what I pay her for. Tell her I sent ya.

NOW BEAT IT!"

"I didn't know you liked punk music," Tim said, looking curiously at Zoe as they walked down the temple stairs. He'd expected she'd be into the ancient equivalent of boy bands, if there was such a thing.

Zoe reddened. "Well, it's a bit of fun, isn't it?"

Tim didn't agree – all that screeching gave him a headache. "Are you going to Apollo's show tonight?"

The girl snorted. "As if Dad would let me buy tickets! He thinks I should be into classical music. He says I'm too young for punk." Her scowl deepened.

Tim quickly changed the subject before she could build up to a really big sulk.

"Right. So we go to Apollo's oracle. I hope it helps." He wasn't so sure anymore – not after meeting Apollo. Still, Zoe's parents thought it was a good idea, and he didn't have a better plan. He looked up and down the street, wondering what an oracle looked like. "Where is it?"

"It's not here," Zoe said, kicking at a pebble. "It's in Delphi. That's miles away."

"Could we find a chariot to take us, do you think?"

"Not without money to pay the driver. There's no way Dad will give us any." Zoe glowered. "You know he won't let me go anywhere."

Tim stood straighter at a sudden idea. "The vase! We'll command the vase to take us."

Zoe's eyes lit up, but quickly clouded over as her gaze shifted to something behind Tim's shoulder. He spun around and saw Hermes standing there, shaking his head.

"The vase won't work for short hops. It can only do long distances through time," the messenger god said, his golden curls catching the sunlight. He jerked his thumb at the black temple. "Been to see

my half-brother, have you? I could've told
you it'd be a waste of time. All he cares
about is blasting everyone's ears with that
stupid lyre of his. Wish I'd never made it
for him now."

"Does that mean we can't get to Delphi?" Tim asked, feeling crestfallen. Without the prophecy, he'd be an easy target for Hera.

Before the god could answer, Zoe butted in.

"What were you doing at Tim's house last night?" she demanded, hand on hip. "Don't deny it – he saw you. Did you plant that flask to trap him?"

Hermes rustled his wings indignantly. "Don't be a twit! I was trying to protect him."

Zoe's eyes narrowed. "How?"

"Hera magicked the lekythos over to Tim Baker's house. You're right, it was a trap. If he brushed against it with his skin, he'd shrink and get sucked inside. I was just moving it out of the way so he wouldn't step on it."

The god's eyes were wide and innocent. He certainly *looked* as if he was telling the truth.

"We can't expect you to tell the truth," Zoe said with a toss of her head, "God of Thieves and Liars."

Hermes sniffed, offended. "All right then, if you don't want me to take you to Delphi, forget it." Wings flapping, he turned and added over his shoulder. "Can't see how else you'll get there, though."

"You can take us?" Tim asked quickly, before the god could fly away.

"Course I can. See these babies?" Hermes pointed at the wings on his hat and sandals. "They can take me anywhere. But if you don't trust me …" He left the sentence hanging in the air.

"We trust you." Tim jumped in before Zoe could disagree. "Please take us. You're our only chance."

"Thanks, buddy." Hermes grinned and held out his hands. Tim grabbed one. Zoe made a sour face but gripped Hermes' other hand. She did it with as much enthusiasm as if she were holding a rotting fish.

"Hold on tight," the god warned them. "Up!" And they went flying through the air.

Traveling with Hermes was very different to riding the vase. Rather than being buffeted by strong winds, it felt like they were walking on clouds. There was no impenetrable golden mist, and Tim was able to watch the scenery unfold. Rocky hills dotted with silvery olive trees sped past faster and faster until they became

a blur. Minutes later, they landed on the side of a rugged mountain.

"Right," Hermes said, releasing them. "That's the Sanctuary of Apollo. You need a tribute before you can see the oracle," Hermes said as they walked along a winding path. "Take one of these each."

He snatched at the air and then opened his palms. One held a small golden flute. In his other hand was a figurine of a punk doubled over vomiting.

Tim chose the flute.

"No attendants today, by the look of it," Hermes said, approaching the temple. It was very quiet and the air was still.

"They're probably getting ready for the gig. The Pythia will be here, though, so we'll go straight to her."

"The who?" Tim asked.

"The Pythia. She's Apollo's oracle. A bit, you know," Hermes twirled a finger around his ear in a *she's nuts* motion. "She's the one everyone comes to when they need advice. Beats me why they bother."

"You wait here," Zoe said bluntly, coming to a halt at the entrance. "This is private. Right, Tim?"

"Wha— Oh, yeah. I guess. If you don't mind," Tim hastened to add. He didn't want Hermes to get offended and leave without them. The Greek gods seemed awfully touchy.

"Whatever." The young god flapped his hands at them. "Just be quick about it. I haven't got all day." He sat on the steps and examined his fingernails moodily.

Clutching their offerings, Zoe and Tim slipped between the soaring columns and entered the heart of the temple. Just as they stepped inside, an unearthly screech filled the air. Tim's blood ran cold.

"What's that noise?" Tim gasped. He tried to block out the horrible screeching by pressing his hands over his ears.

"It's coming from over there." Zoe pointed to a spot deep within the temple's inner chamber. "I think it's a woman."

Tim was shocked. The gurgling, gargling, screaming noise didn't sound remotely human to him. Whoever it was must be in a lot of pain.

"Should we go help her?" he shouted over the noise.

"I think it's the Pythia," Zoe called back. "Let's find her."

If that was the Pythia, Tim couldn't understand why people came to see her. Perhaps they brought earplugs.

The children passed between a row of columns.

"Whoa!" Tim said, confronted by a giant statue of Apollo, at least ten feet tall. Its mohawk bristled aggressively, and its hand was raised in a rude gesture. No Greek statues like that had survived until Tim's day, for which he was grateful. He edged past, unable to tear his gaze away from it.

"Come on," Zoe urged. The children passed through more columns. If anything, the sight that greeted them was even more bizarre.

A young woman was sitting on a three-legged stool. A deep fissure ran through the rocks underneath, and a misty cloud wafted out, enveloping the woman above. A sickly sweet smell drifted toward them. Tim gagged and pinched his nose shut.

"AAIIEEE!"

the woman screeched, pointing at Tim and Zoe. "Aaoo … eee … blaagh!"

Tim didn't know what he'd expected an oracle to look like, but it certainly wasn't this. The Pythia was dressed in a skintight gown. Her arms were covered with leather bracelets that bristled with spiky silver studs. Jet-black hair shaped like spikes poked up all around her head. Tim stared at her open-mouthed. She poked her tongue out at him.

"We've come for a prophecy," Zoe said, stepping forward.

"Garr … ooosh!" the Pythia replied, fixing them with a baleful glare.

Tim thought that the vase's magical translation powers must have stopped working. "What did she say?" he whispered nervously.

"I don't know," Zoe muttered back. "It's gibberish. I've heard she likes to do that." The girl looked back at the oracle and squared her shoulders. "You must give us a prophecy. Apollo himself sent us."

A thoughtful look crossed the Pythia's face. She started swaying, as if to a silent tune.

"A tribute," she croaked, holding out her hand.

"Oh. Right," Tim said, balancing the tiny golden flute on his outstretched palm. Zoe held out the figurine, and the Pythia snatched them both. She examined them carefully, then tossed them into the fissure, which sent up an even larger blast of gas.

"What knowledge do you seek?" the Pythia asked, breathing deeply.

"We have to be careful how we phrase it," Zoe told Tim. "The oracle's known for giving tricky answers. Tell her everything and don't leave anything out."

Tim took his time answering. He told her all about the oil flask. "So what I want to know is," Tim said, "how do I stop Hera from trapping me?"

Tim bit his lower lip as he watched the Pythia sway, eyes closed. For a moment he thought she wasn't going to answer. But then her mouth opened, and a deep echoing voice came out. A man's voice, strangely musical. Tim recognized it as Apollo's.

Listen close and you will hear,
an answer you will surely fear.
The flask is meant to be your tomb
this prophecy is one of doom.
To avoid entrapment in a treasure,
mix wisdom and fire in equal measure.
You've got your answer, so off you jig,
and leave me to my sick punk gig.

"Now go!" the Pythia shouted, suddenly using her own voice again. "Go, go, before I bring the curse of the universe down upon your heads! Aaaeee! Oooo!"

And she started her unearthly screeching again.

Tim and Zoe couldn't get away fast enough.

"Can you remember all that?" Zoe asked once they'd left the temple and were back in the open air.

"I think so," Tim said. "But why's the oracle so mysterious? Can't she just tell us what to do?"

"I dunno. Maybe she's annoyed because she has to work today. She'd probably rather be at the gig."

"We'll see what Hermes thinks," Tim said, looking up and down the street. "If we can find him, that is. Hey, Hermes!" he called. "We're ready to go home."

There was no reply. The sanctuary was deserted.

"He abandoned us!" Zoe's eyes blazed. "I told you not to trust him."

"You shouldn't have been so rude to him," Tim shot back. "Now how will we get home? There's no one here to ask for help. Could we walk?"

"That'll take days!"

Tim thought for a moment. "How about that GGG thing? You know, the Greek God Grapevine. Can't we put out an alert on that?"

Zoe shook her head. "Only gods can do that. You're mortal, and I'm just a quad god."

"Quad god?" Tim was unfamiliar with the expression.

"My dad is a demigod: half man, half god. Mom's mortal. That makes me a quarter of a god – a quad god."

Tim looked at her with interest. "So does that mean you have special powers?"

"If I do, I haven't noticed!" she snapped. "Certainly nothing that could get us home." She threw her arms in the air. "Great! We're stranded."

"Let's try calling Hermes again." Tim couldn't think of anything else to do. "Maybe he went for a stroll and couldn't hear us before."

Zoe clenched her fists but, unable to come up with a better idea, joined Tim in shouting the messenger god's name.

"Keep ya hair on!" The winged god fluttered toward them, looking put out. "Talk about uptight. I got called away to deliver a message, all right?"

Zoe's face twisted. It looked as if the relief of not being abandoned was doing battle with her need to say I told you so. Instead of replying, she tossed her ringlets and sniffed.

"Got your prophecy?" Hermes asked.

"Yes," Tim said, "but it doesn't make sense."

"That's no surprise." Hermes grinned. "Tell me, and I'll see what I can make of it."

Ignoring Zoe's warning look, Tim recited it. He stumbled over the word "tomb."

"Completely nuts, that's what she is," Hermes said after hearing it through. "Trust Apollo to pick a loony as his oracle."

"The Pythia said it was a prophecy of doom." Tim felt a shudder rack his body. "Does that mean there's nothing I can do? I'm going to get trapped, no matter what?"

"Forget the prophecy. It's a load of nonsense," the god said dismissively.

"Oh, is it?" Zoe said, instantly flaring. "Maybe you don't want us to hear anything that might help us!" Tim thought that was unfair. Hermes had been the one who'd taken them to see the oracle, after all.

Hermes looked at the flushed girl and shrugged. "Whatever. But if you want my opinion–"

"We don't," Zoe was quick to say.

"If you want my opinion," Hermes repeated firmly, as if Zoe hadn't spoken, "just keep out of Hera's way. If you're not around, you won't provoke her." It was an echo of Larry's advice.

Tim grimaced. He knew he wasn't safe anywhere, even at home. "What if she puts the flask in my house again?"

"Watch where you step," Hermes said, his face serious. "I've gotta run, more deliveries to make. So if you want a lift …" The god held out his hands. Tim clutched one, eager to walk on air again. Lips pressed into a thin line, Zoe took the other hand.

After another breathtaking flight, Hermes dropped them off at Zoe's house. The children went inside. Tim was hoping to ask Hercules and Agatha what they thought of the prophecy, but the house was empty.

"Let's think before we do anything," Zoe said, picking up a bowl of fruit and offering it to Tim. She sank onto a rug. "It can't all be doom, because the Pythia gave you a way out. What's that line again? *To avoid entrapment in a … erm …*"

"*To avoid entrapment in a treasure, mix wisdom and fire in equal measure,*" Tim recited, selecting a bunch of grapes and sitting next to his friend. "You're right. Why would she say that if there was nothing we could do?"

"Correct." Zoe munched on a fig. "So all we have to do is mix wisdom and fire."

"Oh, is that all?" Tim grimaced. Silence fell as they chewed thoughtfully.

"Have you tried breaking the flask?" Zoe asked eventually.

Tim nodded. "I hit it as hard as I could. It wouldn't break."

"Hmmm."

"Fire," Tim said, thinking aloud. "Maybe we should burn the flask."

"Doesn't that strengthen it? Like, putting a pot in the kiln before you use it?"

"Does it? Hmmm."

"Hmmm."

After a few more minutes of chewing, an idea hit Tim. "That's it! A kiln! We can make our own flask and substitute it for the cursed one! You know, like when Hermes gave your dad a fake copy of my vase so that I could keep the real one." He was referring to the time the hero had supposedly confiscated Tim's magic vase to stop Zoe from joining him on dangerous adventures.

"That could work," Zoe said. "Fire – you light a fire to heat the kiln. And wisdom – meaning you need wisdom to make the flask. That fits the prophecy!"

"Yeah!" Tim said, getting to his feet. "So … err … how do you make a flask?" He was ready to start immediately.

"How would I know?" Zoe gaped up at him.

"You're an Ancient Greek, aren't you? Isn't that what you do?"

"It's a skilled craft," Zoe said slowly, as if Tim were dim. "Not everyone can do it! You'd need to ask a potter and they'd take weeks to make it. And they'd want to be paid. These things aren't cheap."

"There's got to be a way." Tim sank back down onto the rug. "Can we ask Hermes to make it? His fake vase did the job."

"We don't know how he got it. I don't think he could have made it himself. Besides, how can you trust him? He tricked my dad, remember? Why don't we ask Athena? She's the goddess of crafts, you know. I'm sure she can make a flask for us."

"Athena?" Tim shuddered. "Isn't she the one who turned Arachne into a spider? Just because Arachne said she was better at weaving."

"Athena's fine. Really!"

"When she's not busy transforming people! No, she sounds nuts. Isn't she also the goddess of war?" Tim asked, remembering something he'd read.

"Yeah, but in a good way," Zoe said. Tim gave her a blank look, so she sighed and explained: "Athena is the goddess of fair and defensive wars. It's Ares you want to look out for. He's also the god of war, but he's for angry and overly violent battles. Ares is reckless, and Athena's all about strategy."

"I dunno …"

"She's also the goddess of wisdom. As long as we don't challenge her or pretend we're better than her, she'll be okay. Athena's one of the good guys. She gave my dad that owl, remember?"

"Yeah, what's the point of that?" Tim asked, recalling the gigantic toy owl that Hercules had been clutching.

"The owl is Athena's symbol. I don't know why she thought Dad would need it, but I'm sure she had her reasons."

"There was an owl at my window last night," Tim remembered. "You don't think *she* put the flask under my bed, do you?"

"How could she? She can't travel to your day, only Hermes can." Zoe snapped her fingers. "Hey, *wisdom!* Athena's owl is the symbol of wisdom. Like in the prophecy!" She clapped her hands gleefully. "Trust me, Tim. She's the one to see." Zoe jumped up, knocking over the bowl of fruit. "Let's go find her."

Still not convinced they were doing the right thing, Tim let Zoe lead him out of the house and onto the street.

Finding Athena was far easier than Tim
had expected. The goddess was right
outside Zoe's house, as if she knew they
were about to come looking for her.

Tim was surprised by the goddess'
appearance. It was too … normal. After
all the strange people he'd met, Tim
thought that Athena would be strange too.
Instead she was tall and stately, dressed in
a simple white floor-length gown. On her

head was a plumed helmet, pushed back to expose her solemn face. Her gray eyes were clear, and her chin was firm.

"You have need of me?" Athena asked, her voice dignified.

"Err … yes, please." Now that it came down to it, Tim found himself tongue-tied. It was all so complicated. Where should he begin?

He needn't have worried. Zoe launched into a detailed

explanation. She told Athena about the trap that Hera had created and about Apollo's prophecy. By the way the goddess was nodding, Tim thought she already knew all about it.

"The flasks are one and the same," Athena said, answering the question that had puzzled Tim. "The old one in the museum, the new one at your house – the same flask in different moments of time. Both traps."

"Can you make us a copy to substitute for the real thing?" Zoe asked. "One that won't be able to trap Tim, of course."

Athena didn't reply. Instead, she held out her hand, palm facing upward. A silver haze shimmered above her hand. Suddenly an oil flask materialized. It had a loop-shaped handle and a narrow neck. Just like the original, there was a picture of Tim on the front.

"Wow!" Tim said, his eyebrows shooting upward. "That's so cool. But …" He peered at the flask more closely. Something was wrong. "Oh! I shouldn't be wearing a chiton! I should be in my normal clothes."

Athena smiled as the silver mist shimmered over her hand again. When the mist cleared, Tim could see that the picture on the flask had changed. This time, Tim was wearing his too-small fluffy bunny pajamas.

"Not those," he said quickly over Zoe's guffaws. "I mean my school clothes. You know: pants, a shirt …"

But before he could finish describing his uniform, the mist rapidly re-formed and cleared to show Tim dressed correctly. As far as he could tell, this flask was identical to the one he'd discovered in his house.

"Perfect," he said, delighted. "Thank you so much!"

"You are welcome," Athena said gravely, bowing slightly as she offered him the flask. "It is my duty to help heroes in their quests."

"But – but, I'm not a hero," Tim stammered, his face heating up. "I'm just a kid." He gripped the flask carefully with both hands, worried he might drop it.

Athena only smiled at him.

"So now we've got to switch it with the cursed one," Zoe said, thinking ahead. "We'll sneak into Hera's temple and swap them."

Tim didn't like the sound of that. He was grateful when Athena shook her head.

"Too dangerous," the goddess said. "Do the substitution *before* Queen Hera receives the real flask. Before she has a chance to curse it. You must go back in time to the place where her flask was first created."

"What's the point of that?" Tim asked. "Won't Hera still put a curse on the new one?"

"She will try to," Athena said. "And she'll think she's succeeded. But the curse

will fail. I have placed a lock on this flask."
She rapped the lekythos with her knuckles.
"Any curse will bounce off harmlessly, and
Hera will be none the wiser."

"Cool," Tim breathed, looking at Athena
with respect. "But how can we travel
back in time to when the flask was made?
Wasn't it recent?" he asked, suddenly
remembering what Hermes had told him.

"You travel with your vase, of course,"
Athena said.

"I thought it couldn't do short hops."

"Of course it can." Athena's expression
hardened. "Magic is magic. Don't let
anyone tell you otherwise."

Zoe flashed Tim an I-told-you-so
look. Was it possible that Hermes had

been mistaken? Or had he misled them deliberately so that he could eavesdrop on the prophecy?

"Go now," Athena continued. "Fetch your vase. Order it to take you to Epimetheus' workshop, at the moment when the original flask was completed. My blessings go with you." And with a sound like the hooting of an owl, Athena vanished.

■ ■ ■

Tim and Zoe followed Athena's instructions. They found themselves in a vast stone storeroom. The ceiling soared high above them. All four walls were crammed with heavily laden wooden shelves. Every inch of shelf space was taken up with clay pots of various shapes and sizes: vases, drinking cups, oil and perfume flasks. The children scanned the shelves, keen to find Hera's flask before the owner of the workshop turned up. Tim clutched the copy anxiously.

"So who is Epimetheus?" Tim struggled to get his tongue around the unfamiliar name.

"He's a Titan," Zoe said, not taking her eyes off the shelves. "Titans were around before the Olympian gods. Gods and Titans don't exactly get along. It's a long story, but they once had this huge battle that raged for years. They kind of like killing each other."

"WHAT?"

Tim yelped, jumping. "Are you kidding me? You're part god, aren't you? Your grandfather's a god. They might hate you too. We shouldn't be here!"

"Oh, don't worry," Zoe said smoothly. "Epimetheus and his brother joined the Olympians' side. They fought *against* the Titans. So if they catch us, we might be all right."

"Might?" Tim would have preferred something more definite.

"You never can tell with Titans," Zoe replied, moving on to another row. "They get cranky easily. So we'd better stop chattering before they find us."

Frowning, the children went back to their task. All was quiet except for the shuffling of feet as they moved around the workshop.

Finally, Zoe pointed. "It's here!"

"Yep, that's it," Tim agreed. Holding his breath, he picked up the oil flask gingerly. Although it wasn't yet cursed, he still didn't like touching it. Zoe placed the curse-proof copy on the shelf. Now they just had to get the original safely away, and find a way to destroy it.

"Right," Tim said. "Let's grab my vase and–"

But before he could finish his sentence, a booming voice shattered the air.

"INTRUDERS!"

The voice was so loud, the pots rattled on their shelves. "Who dares enter my workshop? When I find you, you'll wish you'd never been created."

There was no time to grab the magic vase and make a break for it. "Quick, hide!" Tim gasped.

"Where?" Zoe's head swiveled from side to side.

The workshop had only one door. The voice had come from that direction, so there was no escape that way. There wasn't even a shady corner to cower in. Their only hope was the storage pots dotted around the room: some looked large enough to climb inside. If they got in and crouched down low, they'd be hidden.

"In those," Tim said, pointing. He hoped the pots weren't already full of something nasty – like boiling oil.

Before they had time to check, however, someone thundered into the workshop. "Aha! Caught you!"

A plump, balding, middle-aged male strode toward them. He wore a brown cloth tied around his waist, exposing a mass of graying chest hairs. His shoulders, arms, and even the backs of his hands were equally hairy. Rather than making him look menacing, however, the grizzled hair softened his appearance.

"Epimetheus," Zoe squeaked, giving a little wave. "Um. Hi!"

"Silence, whoever

you are! Stay right there. Something is amiss – I can feel it." Forehead furrowed in thought, the Titan scanned his overladen shelves, exposing the hairiest back Tim had ever seen. "Aha!" Epimetheus walked straight to the curse-proof flask.

Reaching out with the tips of his fingers, he gripped the flask delicately. Then an incredible thing happened. The flask let out a mouse-like squeak. It rippled and wriggled on the shelf. Then, before their eyes, it leaped to the ground. It rolled around for a while, then scurried into a corner, where it jiggled up and down joyfully. It made a chiming, chuckling sound, as if delighted to find itself alive.

"Not again," Epimetheus grunted.

"What happened?" Tim was stunned.

"Epimetheus used to create animals. He moulded them out of clay, and his touch brought them to life," Zoe said from the corner of her mouth. "He gave each type of animal a unique gift to help it survive. People say he's nice."

The Titan didn't look awfully nice as he turned toward the children. "Who dares to interfere with my work?" he thundered. His bushy eyebrows met in the middle as he frowned down at them.

"M-my name is Tim Baker." He stepped forward, conscious of the fact that he was still holding Hera's flask.

"You dare to steal from me?" the Titan shouted.

"I can explain," Tim said, putting the flask on the floor. He kept his eyes downcast as he explained the story – how Hera was trying to trap him, and how Athena had given him a substitute flask that Hera would be unable to curse.

"How dare she?" Epimetheus thumped his furry fist on a large storage pot. It rolled away, alive and squealing.

Unsure whether the Titan's anger was directed at Hera or at Athena, Tim said nothing.

"Using me as a tool to hurt a child!" Epimetheus shook with rage. "Hera's gone too far this time. That's the last time I make anything for her."

"So – so you're not angry with us?" Tim wanted to be sure.

"Of course not. I love animals and children! I would've preferred you to ask for my help, rather than sneaking in like thieves," Epimetheus said, making Zoe blush, "but you were right to protect yourself." He scratched the stubble on his chin, which rasped like sandpaper. "To be honest, I've never been fond of Hera. Not after what her husband did to my brother."

"What did he do?" Tim asked.

"I'll let him tell you himself," Epimetheus said darkly. "Hey! Prometheus!" he called. "Some children to see you."

While they waited, Tim looked at the Titan curiously. "Does everything you touch come to life?" The large storage pot was now giving the flask a piggyback ride. Both giggled happily.

"Only if I'm not paying attention," Epimetheus said with a sigh. "The world's getting so crowded, Prometheus and I try not to create any new species. We restrict ourselves to simple ceramics now. Of course, my brother's the one who really started the overcrowding problem by creating humans."

Tim jumped. "He did what?"

"You're welcome," a sour voice said. A skinny, stooped man entered the room. Unlike his brother, his skin was smooth and hairless. It had an unhealthy yellow tinge, though, and he rubbed his abdomen as if it pained him. "Yes, I created your kind. Sometimes I regret it."

"Don't be like that–" Epimetheus started, but his brother cut across him.

"We ran out of gifts, thanks to him." Prometheus jerked his thumb at Epimetheus. "He never thinks ahead! He'd already given away all the horns, tusks, stingers, and fangs

– the things we like to give our creations so that they can defend themselves. By the time I got around to

making humans, there was nothing left. So I had to … well … 'borrow' a few things."

"Like what?" Zoe asked, pursing her lips in disapproval.

"Wisdom from Athena. Fire from Hephaestus."

Tim's heart leaped in his chest. Wisdom and fire! The prophecy! They had to be on the right track.

"Mere trifles." Prometheus waved his hand as if shooing away a fly. "The punishment Zeus inflicted on me! You wouldn't believe it."

"What did he do?"

"Zeus chained him to a cliff and set eagles to peck at his liver." Zoe answered Tim's question. "Whenever his liver grew back, eagles would peck it out again. My dad told me," she added before anyone could ask. "He's the one who rescued you," she added to Prometheus.

"Hercules?" For the first time, the hint of a smile crossed the Titan's face. "You are the daughter of Hercules?"

Zoe nodded.

"Then I shall help you! Without your father, I would still be in chains." Prometheus grimaced and rubbed his abdomen. "So – what do you need? Some more wisdom, perhaps? I think I've still got some left."

"In a way," Tim said. Then, for what felt like the tenth time that day, he described his problem.

Prometheus listened to Tim's story with mounting anger. "Hera!" he spat. "She's as bad as her husband! Let's try to fix the copy. I'm not really up to it, mind … still quite sore … my liver … my back … all aching … but we can't let Hera get away with this."

Zoe looked dubiously at the flask, which was playing hide and seek with the storage pot. "Don't hurt it!"

"Might I make a suggestion?" Epimetheus interrupted, his eyebrows lowered.

"To bring me a chair? Something to get the weight off my feet?" Prometheus said gratefully. "That's jolly thoughtful of you. And here I was thinking that you didn't care."

"No, my brother. It's something far more important," Epimetheus said gently. "I do not wish to take life away from the curse-proof flask. Look at the innocent creature. It wouldn't be right."

Tim agreed. There had to be another way.

"So why don't we create a way for Tim Baker to escape from the original flask if he is captured?" Epimetheus continued.

"Like what?" Tim asked.

The Titan scratched his head. "To get in, you must first be shrunk, right? So maybe we could put a tiny ladder inside the flask. You can use it to climb out."

Prometheus clicked his tongue. "That wouldn't work. Hera could simply look inside and see it. No, we need something smarter, something undetectable. If only my feet didn't hurt so much … it would be easier to think … if I could rest them perhaps …"

Sighing, Epimetheus left the room. He returned a few moments later carrying a chair and a footstool. He set them up, then guided his groaning brother toward them.

"Ah, that's better, thank you,"
Prometheus said, putting up his feet. "And
my liver tonic?"

Face set, Epimetheus left the room
again and returned with a steaming cup.
It smelled like some sort of herbal tea.
They all waited while Prometheus slurped
noisily.

"Well?" Epimetheus asked, the hairs on
his arms bristling. "Any bright ideas?"

"Yes, of course," Prometheus said. "It
won't work, though."

Zoe's face was downcast, but Tim was
curious. "What is it? What's your idea?"

Prometheus sipped his tea again before
answering. "We could bore a small hole
in the flask and seal it with wax. We'd

do such a good job, the hole would be
invisible. Then if Tim were ever caught,
he could melt the wax and escape through
the hole." The Titan mopped his brow, as
if exhausted from his long speech. "But as
the boy cannot make fire unaided …"

"I can!" Tim said, jumping. "I can carry
a box of matches!"

It took time for him to explain what matches were, what they looked like, and how they worked. Tim wasn't quite sure about the last bit, but somehow he managed to explain it to the Titans' satisfaction.

"Excellent," Prometheus said. He sounded proud. "Humans have made good use of the wisdom I gave them! We shall do this at once. Hera's coming today to collect her flask. She'll have no idea what we've done. Give it to my brother."

Tim picked up the original flask and handed it over.

"Don't come to life, don't come to life," Epimetheus muttered under his breath as he transferred the flask to a work bench.

"It's best if you leave now, children, before Hera turns up. Remember to always carry those magic fire sticks, Tim Baker."

"I will!" Tim said with feeling. "I'll keep a matchbox in my pocket everywhere I go."

"Perhaps you could bring some for me," Prometheus said, looking up hopefully. "I'm sure they would ease my pain. I can still make fire, of course, but rubbing sticks together is a lot of effort. My back hurts, you know … and sometimes my legs … these fire sticks would make life so much easier …"

"I can't give you something from the future," Tim said, wringing his hands. "It might change history."

"Of course it would," Epimetheus agreed. "My brother would only try to gift them to humans again. And what would Zeus do then? No, off you go, children. Be sure to send your father our regards, Zoe."

"Thank him from me," Prometheus said as the children picked up the vase. They promised that they would. Then they were enveloped in a golden haze.

■ ■ ■

The vase deposited the children outside Zoe's house. Tim could hear Hercules' loud voice booming across the courtyard. "Why is she not back yet? Has something happened? Perhaps a flock of Stymphalian birds is eating her at this very moment!"

Rolling her eyes, Zoe pushed the door open. "I'm here," she called. "I'm not being eaten by anything."

"Thank the gods," said Hercules, his voice shaking. He strode to the door and lifted his daughter over the threshold.

"Let the boy in, dear," said Agatha. "You're filling up the doorway."

"Oh. Right." Hercules turned sideways to make room for Tim to pass.

Before Tim could enter, a yowling, growling noise came from behind him. A shiver ran down his back. He recognized that sound. Spinning around, he turned to face the street. His suspicions were right. The area was filling up with peacocks. Fanning

139

their tales and squawking loudly, they looked as savage as guard dogs.

Tim knew what the birds' presence meant. The peacocks were calling their mistress, Queen Hera. And when they called, the goddess was sure to appear.

It only took a moment for Hera to appear.
In a golden flash, the goddess materialized
among her peacocks. "Settle, petals. I am
here," Hera said to her birds, raising her
hands in a soothing gesture. "Do not be
agitated. I have come to end this, once and
for all."

Tim saw that Hera was holding the
cursed flask. It felt as if someone had
poured ice water down his back. He

shivered. Did the flask contain the wax-covered escape hole? It must! In his short hop to the past, Epimetheus had promised he would add it before Hera was due to pick up the flask. Unless she turned up unexpectedly early, and the Titan didn't get the chance …

"I told you never to come near my family again!" Hercules roared, towering in the doorway.

"LEAVE MY HOME AT ONCE."

His sheer bulk blocked Hera from entering the house, where Zoe and Agatha stood huddled together. Zoe peeped out from around her father's elbow, a look of horror in her eyes. She was probably remembering what it had been like to be trapped in that giant puzzle prison.

"I care not for your brat," Hera said, sneering at Zoe. "I have come for her troublesome companion. This boy is not of our time. He cares nothing about our ways."

"Don't believe her, Dad." Zoe gripped her father's arm. "She's after you!"

"I am prepared to make a deal," Hera spat. "Give me Timothy Baker, and I will leave you and your family alone."

"And if I refuse?" Hercules said.

"Then I shall take your daughter instead! Choose. Where do your loyalties lie? With your child, or with this strange boy from another time?"

Tim held his breath. He was only feet away from the angry goddess and her peacocks. Hercules stood between Tim and the safety of the house. The hero stood motionless, not making way for Tim to enter.

"Let him in," Zoe urged. Agatha added her agreement.

Twisting around, Tim could see the conflict etched on Hercules' face. If the hero moved, he would expose his daughter to Hera's wrath. If he didn't, Tim was doomed. Tim opened and closed his mouth, not sure what to say. How could he ask Hercules to risk everything for him?

"I am warning you, Hera." Hercules' voice shook. "Leave now or I shall—"

"Shall what?" Hera said silkily. "Eat a honey cake at me? You oaf, haven't you learned yet? There is nothing you can do to hurt me. Now hand him over, and I promise that your brat will be safe."

Tim felt Hercules shake with indecision. "Tim Baker, I do not know what to do." Tim could hear the agony in the hero's voice.

Furious, Tim spun around to face Hera. It was all her fault that his friends were upset. He glowered at the goddess and clenched his fists. If only he had a mobile phone to threaten her with!

Hera flinched and took a step backward.

Tim blinked. Was he imagining it, or did she look frightened?

"Don't trust her," Zoe begged. "She'll try to catch us all no matter what we do! So let Tim in and then …" Her voice died away.

And then what? If the hero moved aside to let Tim in, what would happen next? Would Hera seize the chance to snatch Zoe or Agatha? Could Tim live with himself if she succeeded?

"Th-that's all right," he stammered. "Leave the others alone. I'll go to Hera."

"Are you crazy?" Zoe hissed from the doorway. "She's got the flask!"

"The escape hole," Tim murmured softly, so that Hera wouldn't hear. Yes, it would be awful if Hera trapped him. But the moment she looked away, confident that Tim was imprisoned forever, he'd be able to melt the wax by using his–

The realization hit him at the same time that Zoe hissed, "You don't have any matches yet!"

"Oh. Yeah." Tim gulped. He smiled weakly.

Hera seemed unaware of their whispered discussion. She thrust the flask toward Tim, her slender arms shaking ever so slightly. "Come to me now, Timothy Baker. Come to meet your doom!"

Tim wavered, unsure what to do – when suddenly everything happened at once.

At a signal from Hera, half a dozen peacocks rushed at Hercules and Tim. Catching him off guard, the birds pecked at Tim's legs, drawing blood. Hera lunged at Tim, thrusting the flask at his face. She missed by inches.

At the same time, a loud flapping of wings sounded from behind him. He turned in confusion.

More peacocks? But the noise was coming from *inside* Zoe's house! Had they somehow got in?

"Duck!" Zoe shouted. She tugged on Hercules' arm as she dropped to the floor.

The hero stumbled and slammed to the ground. Tim's arms pinwheeled as he

struggled to retain his balance. Just when
he thought he'd manage to stay on his feet,
something big swept out of the house and
knocked Tim over with a *whump*. It felt
like he'd been whacked by a giant feather
duster. Wings flapped near his exposed

head, and he covered his face with his hands. His legs were already oozing blood; it was only a matter of time before they went for his eyes.

14

The noises around Tim changed. The peacocks' squawking turned from anger to fear. Some whimpered, like dogs in pain.

"No!" Hera shouted, furious. "Leave my petals alone."

Risking a pecking, Tim peered out from between his fingers. What he saw made his jaw drop in disbelief.

A giant owl was swooping over the peacocks, dive-bombing them. It must have been the owl that had knocked him to the ground, Tim realized. His eyes bulged as they followed its flight. The owl was identical to the cuddly toy that Athena had given Hercules. Had it come to life? The owl swooped and soared before dropping and rising again. Hera's peacocks scattered, all the fight frightened out of them.

"STOP IT AT ONCE."

Hera stamped her foot. "How dare you interfere?"

Was she talking to the owl? Tim sat up in confusion. The big bird tucked in its wings and dived. It looked like it was about to smash itself into the ground. Before it hit, however, the owl vanished into a silver mist. Athena appeared in its place, standing tall and serene.

"It is my duty to interfere." Just like the last time they had met the goddess, her helmet was pushed back off her face. This time, however, Athena was holding a spear and a shield. Her face was grim and her gray eyes were hard as stone.

"It is not!" Hera snapped. "This is none of your business."

"Oh, but it is. I am the protector of heroes." Athena reached down and pulled Tim gently to his feet. Sidestepping him, she positioned herself so that she stood between Tim and Hera.

"That squirt?" Hera shrieked, pointing at him. "He is not a hero! He's nothing but a scared brat. See how he quivers in his sandals?"

"Yet he was willing to sacrifice himself to protect his friends," Athena said. "To my way of thinking, that qualifies him as a hero."

"Your 'way of thinking,'" Hera echoed in a mocking voice. "You think you're so smart. You should never have been made goddess of wisdom. It's gone to your head! Goddess of fools, that is what you are!"

Athena did not respond to the taunts. She stood firm.

Hera stamped her foot again. "I do not wish to fight with you, sister goddess. If you have wisdom, accept that this boy from another time is not worth a battle between gods. Stand aside. Allow me to dispose of this threat." She waved the flask in the air.

"And if I do not?" Athena's voice was mild, but she was already lowering her helmet in preparation.

"I shall make you." Pale eyes flashing, Hera twisted her free hand in the air as if she were turning a doorknob. A large, dark-red sphere appeared in her grip.

"Uhhh," Tim recognized the object. It was a pomegranate – the fruit that Zoe had once told him was Hera's symbol. Like the peacocks, Hera had turned them into weapons. In a previous adventure, she had hurled pomegranates at Tim and Zoe, and they'd exploded like hand grenades. "Watch out!" he shouted to Athena.

Her expression like ice, Hera pulled back her arm and hurled the pomegranate with all her might. Without fuss,

Athena held out her spear, impaling the fruit neatly. In one smooth motion, she swung it toward Hercules.

"Excellent," he murmured. Tim twisted around to see the hero pluck the fruit off the end of the spear and suck eagerly at its ruby juices.

Undaunted, Hera hurled another pomegranate in their direction. This one was heading straight at them. Tim closed his eyes as it whirred through the air. There was a wet smacking sound and Tim opened his eyes again in time to see the fruit explode. Seeds whizzed in all directions, but Tim and his friends were protected by Athena's shield.

"Aargh!" Tim heard Hera shriek.

Tim looked over at the queen goddess. Hera was covered head to foot in red streaks. Tim gasped. Was that blood? Had she been hit by her own shrapnel? She certainly sounded like she was in a lot of pain.

"My gown!" Hera cried. "You've ruined my beautiful gown! Do you know how difficult it is to get pomegranate juice out of fine clothes?"

Tim found himself breathing a sigh of relief. It wasn't blood. Just juice.

Hera glared at Athena, looking her up and down with contempt. "Obviously you don't. You have the dress sense of a common soldier. And look at my petals!" The goddess' voice grew even more shrill as she looked at her peacocks, who were also covered in juice. "How do you expect me to clean their feathers?"

"If your gown is ruined, I can recommend a good weaver," Athena said, smiling. "Have you ever heard of Arachne?"

"Very funny. You have not seen the last of me!" Hera stormed.

And with a click, Hera, the flask, and the peacocks disappeared.

"Hera fears you, Tim Baker," Athena said, accepting a honey cake from Agatha. Now that Hera had gone, they were all sitting around enjoying the feast that Agatha had insisted on preparing. Athena took an appreciative bite of the cake. "Mmm, these are very good."

"Thank you," Agatha replied, bowing her head. "Of course they are not nearly as good as yours."

Tim nodded. That was smart thinking. Athena might be magnificent, but she had an unfortunate tendency to turn people who challenged her skills into spiders.

"Why is she afraid of Tim?" Zoe asked, noisily spitting out an olive pit, which earned her a frown from her mother.

"He's from the future," the goddess replied. "It is unknown to us. Hera fears what the future may bring."

Tim remembered how apprehensive Hera had become when Larry whipped out his mobile phone. The queen goddess seemed to believe Larry's bluff that he could trap people inside his phone, when all he'd been doing was showing her a video of Mom he'd recorded.

"Why should she, though?" Tim wondered out loud. "I mean, why should she care what happens thousands of years in the future? She's Queen of Mount Olympus *now*. Isn't that enough?"

Athena, who'd removed her helmet and laid it beside her, shook her head. "It's not enough for Hera. She fears being forgotten. She fears becoming obsolete. This is the curse of immortality." Athena

frowned. "Hera wants the world to stay exactly as it is today. Are we still worshipped in your day, Tim Baker? Are there people who follow us still?"

Tim broke his gaze away from Athena's cool gray eyes. How could he tell her that, not only were they no longer worshipped, no one even believed in them anymore? Most people thought the gods of Olympus were myths. He didn't want to

hurt her feelings, and he certainly didn't want to anger her.

"Umm, well, I'd have to say—"

"That means no." Athena pressed her lips together. For a moment she looked sad. Shaking herself, she picked up another honey cake and nodded. "That is to be expected. Everything has its time. Change must happen for the world to progress. Is that not so, Hercules?" Athena turned to the hero. "You have resided in the future. Is the world prosperous without us?"

Hercules, who had been steadily filling his face with food, nodded, his cheeks bulging. "They have lots of good snacks. The potato chips are excellent."

"There you are then," Athena said comfortably. "Hera would do well to focus on the here and now. I shall remind her of that at the earliest opportunity." Sighing, she picked up her helmet, spear, and shield. "It's time for me to depart."

"Um, before you go, can I ask you something?" Tim said shyly. When the goddess nodded, he continued. "Last night, when I was in my bed, I heard an owl at my window. I was wondering, was that ..."

"Me? How could it be? I can't time travel." She smiled down at Tim. "Goodbye, my heroic friend. I shall be watching your adventures with interest." And, with the sound of an owl hooting, the goddess vanished.

"Wow, Tim," Zoe breathed. "She called you a hero!"

"I don't get it," Tim said, his tired brain feeling muddled. "If it wasn't her, then why did an owl wake me up when Hermes was there? Was it a coincidence?"

Agatha smoothed down Tim's hair. "Just as Hera can control peacocks and bend them to her will, Athena can control owls. My guess is that she projected her will into an owl in your world. She made it hoot out a warning."

"She must be very powerful to reach that far," Tim said, stifling a massive yawn. Last night's broken sleep had caught up with him.

"She is," Agatha agreed. "But – hero or not – you still need your sleep. I think it's best if you go home now, Tim Baker. It'll be night when you go back – yes? You can return whenever you like after you have rested."

"Oh, Ma," Zoe started.

Tim couldn't help but agree. The adrenaline that had surged through his body had gone, leaving him feeling limp and washed out. He knew that the vase would take him home to a time just moments after he'd left. A sleep in his own bed sounded marvelous. Yawning, he stood up and collected his vase.

"Your clothes," Agatha reminded Tim, handing him the pajamas he'd been wearing when he'd time-jumped. "Leave your chiton here, ready for your next visit. Unless you prefer to wear this again." She pointed at a fluffy bunny, and Zoe dissolved into a fit of giggles.

■　■　■

The next morning, Tim awoke in his own room, feeling disoriented. Had last night actually happened? Had the goddess

Athena really called him a hero? He'd fallen asleep so soon after his return that the adventure had a dream-like quality. There was only one way to know for sure …

Tim clambered out of bed, checking the ground was clear before swinging his feet to the floor. Getting down on his hands and knees, he peered under the bed. The flask was still there, tucked out of reach.

So it *was* real – the flask, the adventure – everything.

He dithered, unsure what to do about the flask under his bed. Maybe it had the escape hole, maybe it didn't. Either way, Tim decided the flask was best left exactly where it was, where it could do no harm. He made a mental note to borrow a box of Mom's candle-lighting matches as soon as possible.

"C'mon, sleepy head! You slept through your alarm." Mom bustled into his room, already dressed for work. "What are you doing on the floor?"

"Err …"

"Hurry up. Breakfast, then school. You're getting your project today, remember? The grades are going on your report card. You don't want to miss that."

Pulling himself to his feet, Tim suddenly grinned. Life was good. A goddess had called him a hero. Hera was frightened of the future, a weakness that Tim would keep in mind. And Agatha had told him to come back as soon as he liked. Nothing – not even homework – could dampen his day.

Or so he thought.

At school, Miss Omiros described their project. "You're going to design and build a raft," she said, "and it has to float! All successful rafts will be entered in a race and the winners will get a special prize. This is for homework, remember, and you'll work in pairs."

Tim and Ajay exchanged a look across the classroom. They worked well together. It would be fun to go to each other's houses to make a raft. And Ajay's father was an engineer – they'd as good as won the race already!

"Ajay, you team up with Rania."

Tim felt deflated, but there was nothing he could do about it. He wasn't going to let anything spoil his day. Miss Omiros walked up and down the room, pairing people up.

"Tim, you're with Leo." She breezed past as if she hadn't just made the worst announcement in the world.

Tim felt his stomach sink to his feet.

"Can't wait to come to your house.
I've always wanted to see what it's like
inside." Leo thrust his face close to Tim's
and sneered. "I know you've got a secret.
And guess what? I'm gonna find out what
you're hiding. I'm on to you, Cinders!"

Look out for Tim's next adventure...

COMING SOON.

HOPELESS HEROES

JASON'S WILD WINDS!

STELLA
TARAKSON

Sweet
Cherry
PUBLISHING

1

"Oh no, not again!" Tim Baker watched his model raft slide under the water's surface and hit the bottom of the bathtub. He

dunked a hand into the water and fished the dripping raft out, glaring at it. That was the tenth time it had sunk. He'd tried everything: changing the length of the twigs, the width of the twigs, how he tied them together, the type of string he used. Nothing worked. No matter what he did, the stupid thing kept sinking. The last thing Tim needed was another **F** at school.

Frowning, he sank onto his knees beside the tub. It might've helped if Leo had bothered to turn up! They were meant to be doing the project together. Not that they wanted to be paired up – Miss Omiros had forced them to work together. It was now late Sunday afternoon. The project was due tomorrow, and Tim had been struggling on his own all weekend. The bully expected Tim to do all the work, but would still take a share of the glory.

TYPICAL!

Except … it was becoming clear that there'd be no glory. The raft kept sinking, and Tim was out of ideas on how to fix it.

Pain flared in his jaw and Tim grimaced. The toothache that had started as a mild twinge a few days ago was becoming stronger. More frequent, too. He knew he ought to tell Mom, but she would insist on a visit to the dentist. Enough said.

Tim glowered at the raft as if it were to blame. Putting it on the floor, he resisted the urge to kick it. Just then, the doorbell rang. He heard Mom open the front door and call out, "Tim, your friend's here!"

Did she mean Ajay? Feeling cheered, Tim ran down the stairs. Knowing him, Ajay's raft would be already finished. Maybe he could give Tim a few pointers. But the sight that greeted Tim through the doorway stopped him in his tracks.

On the doorstep stood Leo and an angry-looking old woman. Tim

recognized her as the bully's grandmother.
Her gray hair was pulled back in a
bun that was as severe as her scowl.
Her wrinkled hands clutched at Leo's
shoulders like an eagle's talons.

"Now get in
there and do
your project," the
woman growled,
pushing him over
the threshold.
"Don't come home
before it's done –
or I'll fix you up!"

"Yes, Grandma,"
Leo said, his head
bowed. The boy's

face was red, and he kept his gaze on the floor as he clumped up the stairs and followed Tim into the bathroom.

Embarrassed, Tim said nothing. He could see the look of misery on Leo's face. His eyes were watery and red-rimmed. Had he been crying? It didn't seem possible, not given how tough Leo always acted. And what was that phrase his grandma had used? "Fix you up"? That's what Leo kept threatening to do to Tim!

"Um," Tim said eventually, needing to break the awkward silence. He dragged his gaze away from the boy's face. "I haven't had much luck with the raft. It keeps sinking."

Leo shrugged his beefy shoulders.

"Whaddya expect me to do about it?"

"Do you know how to fix it?" Tim decided to ignore the aggression in Leo's voice.

"Why would I?"

"I just thought you might have an idea. I asked my mom but she didn't know." Tim could have asked Mom's boyfriend Larry, who was a teacher at their school, but he wanted to show him that he could do things on his own. "Hey, how about your parents? Would your mom or dad know what to do?"

"NO."

Leo's answer was abrupt.

"Have you asked them?"

The boy clenched his fists. "No."

"Why not?" Tim persisted. "It wouldn't hurt to ask, would it? Maybe you can ring them up–"

"I don't have parents," Leo said through gritted teeth. "Happy now?"

"Sorry," Tim mumbled, feeling his own cheeks turn red. He didn't want to pursue the matter, but he was beginning to realize that Leo's home life wasn't awfully happy. He might even understand him a little bit better now. Tim's own father had died when he was little, but Tim's mother had never let him feel unloved. He was also grateful for his friendship with the hero Hercules. Although the demigod lived in Ancient Greece, Tim could go and see him whenever he liked.

Tim had first met Hercules when he accidentally broke an old Greek vase that the hero had been trapped in. By repairing the vase and solving the riddle on it, Tim was able to send the hero back home. Since then, Tim had been using the vase to travel to and from Ancient Greece. There he'd befriended Hercules' daughter Zoe, and together they'd had many adventures, encountering dangerous creatures and trying to escape the wicked goddess Hera.

Tim had also met many

interesting – if somewhat bizarre –
people. People like Theseus the vain heart-
throb, Perseus the flower fanatic, and
Jason the boat builder.

Tim started.

JASON!

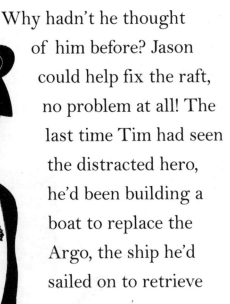

Why hadn't he thought
of him before? Jason
could help fix the raft,
no problem at all! The
last time Tim had seen
the distracted hero,
he'd been building a
boat to replace the
Argo, the ship he'd
sailed on to retrieve

190

the Golden Fleece. A model raft would be nothing to him!

"I've got an idea." Tim scooped up the raft and looked at Leo. "Stay here, I'll be right back," he said, as he ran out of the room.

Tim dashed into his bedroom where he kept the magic vase. He opened the wardrobe door and whipped off the sheet covering the large Greek amphora. Knowing it would bring him back before Leo even noticed he was gone, Tim grabbed the big black handles.

"Oh vase," he said, "take me to Jason and the *Argonut*."

Tim held on tight as the vase took him soaring through time and space, the now-

familiar golden mist
glittering around his body.
He hoped the vase would take him
to a time when Jason had finished building
his new boat, the *Argonut*. Otherwise he'd
be too busy with his own work to have
time for Tim's raft.

Tim expected to land at Jason's home,
where they'd met before. Tim and Zoe
had been searching for the Golden
Fleece, only to have Jason tell them
he'd given it to his girlfriend, Arachne.
Unknown to the boat-obsessed Jason,
Arachne had been turned into a giant
spider, who had woven the fleece into
a pair of gloves. Luckily it had kept
its magical healing properties, and the

children were able to rescue the people who'd been turned to stone by the snake-haired gorgon. Since then, Tim had vowed to always keep the gloves with him in case he ever needed them again … but most of the time he forgot. Like now.

He made a mental note to remember them next time, but it promptly fled his mind when he touched solid ground. This was not Jason's house! The vase had brought Tim to a place he'd never been before. Grappling with the raft and the unwieldy vase, Tim gazed at his surroundings.

He was standing at the edge of a vast, glittering ocean. A fresh, salty smell filled the air and a light wind whipped around his face. A few feet away, at the end of an old wharf, stood a shiny new boat. A young man was waxing it lovingly. He had closely shaven hair with a long tuft on top.

He was so engrossed in his work that he didn't look around when Tim approached.

"Jason?" Tim tried to get his attention. "We've met before, remember? I'm Tim Baker."

Jason grunted but otherwise ignored him.

"My friend and I were looking for the fleece," Tim tried again. "And you told us–"

"Hold this, will ya?" Without turning his head, Jason thrust a cloth at Tim.

"Um, sure." Tim put the vase down so he could grab the cloth. "As I was saying–"

"How do you like my new ride?" Jason spoke over him. "Isn't she awesome?"

"Err …" Suddenly, Tim remembered. The only way to get Jason's attention was to imitate the way he talked and – more importantly – praise his boat. "None finer, bro," Tim said. He was kind of relieved that Zoe wasn't there to laugh at him.

"For real? Cool." Jason finally looked at him. "I know you, don't I? Hey, yeah. You're the little bro who was asking me about her buoyancy." Jason patted the boat as it bobbed up and down in the water. "The only way to know for sure is to test her out, which I'm just about to do. I've been looking forward to this moment forever, ya know?"

"I hear ya." Tim nodded solemnly.

The sail caught a gust of air and billowed, as if the boat itself were growing impatient.

"She's all set up and raring to go. Much as I'd love to hang around and chat, I can't wait anymore." Jason turned and cast an eager glance at the boarding plank. "Catch ya later."

"NO! WAIT!"

Tim's voice was more shrill than he intended.

"You wanna come along?" Jason asked, looking over his shoulder at Tim. "I don't mind, long as you're quick."

"No. Well, yes." It would be fun, come to think of it. But Tim didn't want to forget the purpose of his visit. "I wanted to ask you a favor first. Can you please fix my raft?"

But Jason already had one foot on the

plank. "What, you mean now? Don't think so, bro."

"But-but, you're so good at it," Tim said beseechingly. "It wouldn't take long and no one else is as good at making boats as you are. Err … bro."

Jason couldn't help looking pleased at the compliment. "Oh go on then. Give it here. Long as it's quick."

Spirits rising, Tim thrust the raft at the boat builder.

Jason hemmed and hawed as he turned it over in his hands.

"Well here's your problem!" he said after a moment. "The mast is way too long, and it's totally in the wrong place." Snorting in disbelief, he threw the raft into the sea, where it promptly plummeted to the bottom. "Little bro, what were you thinking? Gimme my kit."

Tim rushed to pick up the satchel that Jason was pointing at. The hero dug around and extracted offcuts of wood, cloth and pieces of string. Tim watched in awed silence as a small, sleek boat started to form in Jason's hands. His fingers moved quickly and confidently. He made a mast and sail and deftly secured the whole thing together.

"There ya go," Jason said, holding out an exact replica of the Argonut and grinning.

"Wow, thank you!" Tim took the model boat reverently. "That looks amazing.

Does it float?"

"Course it does. Now are you coming for a ride or what? You can help work the sail."

Tim was tempted. He'd never been on a boat before. And to actually go sailing with *the* Jason from Jason and

the Argonauts … it was too good an opportunity to pass up!

"I'd love to," Tim said, quickly making up his mind. "What do I do with my stuff?" He nodded at his vase.

"Give it here," Jason said, and stowed the vase securely on the boat. "And that." He took the model out of Tim's hands and tucked it next to the vase. "Come on, let's ride."

Tim couldn't help thinking about Zoe, however, who had a constant yearning for adventure. "Can my friend come too? She'd absolutely love to …"

"You mean that bossy chick?" Jason clearly remembered their last encounter. "She's Hercules' daughter, right?" He scratched his head contemplatively. "Yeah, better bring her along or Herc will complain that I upset her. But be quick or I'm going without ya!"

"I'll be quick," Tim agreed. He turned to leave, then stopped. "Um … which way do I go?"

●　●　●

Repeating Jason's directions to himself, Tim ran toward Zoe's house.

"Someone's in a hurry," a figure muttered as Tim darted by.

Not slowing down, Tim turned his head and flashed an apologetic grin. It was Hermes, the messenger god. The wings on his cap and sandals fluttered in greeting.

"Sorry-in-a-rush!" Tim panted.

"How come?" Hermes called after him.
Tim pretended that he hadn't heard.
He picked up his pace. Long explanations
would only delay him, and besides, he was
starting to think that Zoe
might be right. Maybe
they shouldn't trust
Hermes. Although
he acted friendly,
Hermes was

Hera's servant, as well as being the god of thieves and liars. But this wasn't the time to worry about it. It was time to grab his friend and have some fun.

Tim found the right house and knocked on the door. It was flung open before he'd finished knocking. Standing there, wringing her hands, was Zoe's mother.

"Where is she? Where's Zoe?" Agatha asked, her voice tight with anxiety. Tim stared at her in surprise. Normally Agatha was cool, calm, and in control. Unlike her husband Hercules, she was softly spoken and thoughtful. Today, however, there was a tremble in her voice. Her normally sleek hair was tumbling out of its braid, and there were dark circles under her eyes.

Tim was so taken aback it took him a moment to work out what Agatha was saying. "Y-you mean Zoe's missing?" he stammered, aghast. "When? What happened?"

HOPELESS HEROES

To download Hopeless Heroes

ACTIVITIES
AND
POSTERS

visit:
www.sweetcherrypublishing.com/resources

Sweet
Cherry
PUBLISHING